CANDLE'S GREAT FEAST

Kristina Lahr

Illustrated by Virginia de la Lastra

LUMINARE PRESS
WWW.LUMINAREPRESS.COM

SPECIAL NOTE:

The design of the church in this book is based on Iglesia San Francisco de Borja in Santiago, Chile, which was looted and burned by protesters in 2020. May our Blessed Mother Mary protect all persecuted Christians.

CANDLE'S GREAT FEAST
Copyright © 2021 by Kristina Lahr

All rights reserved. This book or any portion thereof may not be reproduced or used in any manner whatsoever without the express written permission of the publisher, except for the use of brief quotations in a book review.

Printed in the United States of America

Cover Design by Virginia de la Lastra and Kristen Brack
Illustrated by Virginia de la Lastra

Luminare Press
442 Charnelton St.
Eugene, OR 97401
www.luminarepress.com

LCCN: 2021900786
ISBN: 978-1-64388-592-6

For our Lord Jesus Christ in the Eucharist

There was once a candle shop on a busy street. In the back of the store on the bottom shelves stood the plainest candles. Each day customers praised and bought the fancy candles around them.

"How lovely this smells!" a customer said of a lavender candle.

"This beautiful color will match my tablecloth perfectly!" said another.

Day after day, the plain candles watched the fancy candles leave the store.

"We shall never light a dinner!" they wailed, "or match a tablecloth. We shall remain here forever. Always dark. Always forgotten."

But one candle, who lived in the deepest, darkest corner of the shelf, couldn't even see the fancy candles. He longed to see what was beyond his shelf but could only listen to the voices of the candles, the customers, and to his heart that longed for more.

"Someday I will light a great feast," he said. "I will light a table for kings, queens, and servants alike. All will be invited, and the music and singing will never end."

But the other candles said, "There is no such feast. Even if there was, the other candles would be chosen before any of us. Why hope for something that will never happen?"

One day, the candle in the deepest, darkest corner heard the voice of a man, as clear as could be.

"I will take 50 of these," he said.

The candles cheered! One by one, the priest and the shop owner gathered the plain candles into a box.

"1, 2, 3, 4..."

"36, 37, 38, 39..."

The candle in the deepest, darkest corner
saw light for the first time.

"There is hope!" he said. "I will light the feast!
There is hope. There is hope. There is—"

"48, 49, 50."

He was not chosen. Every single candle was taken but him.

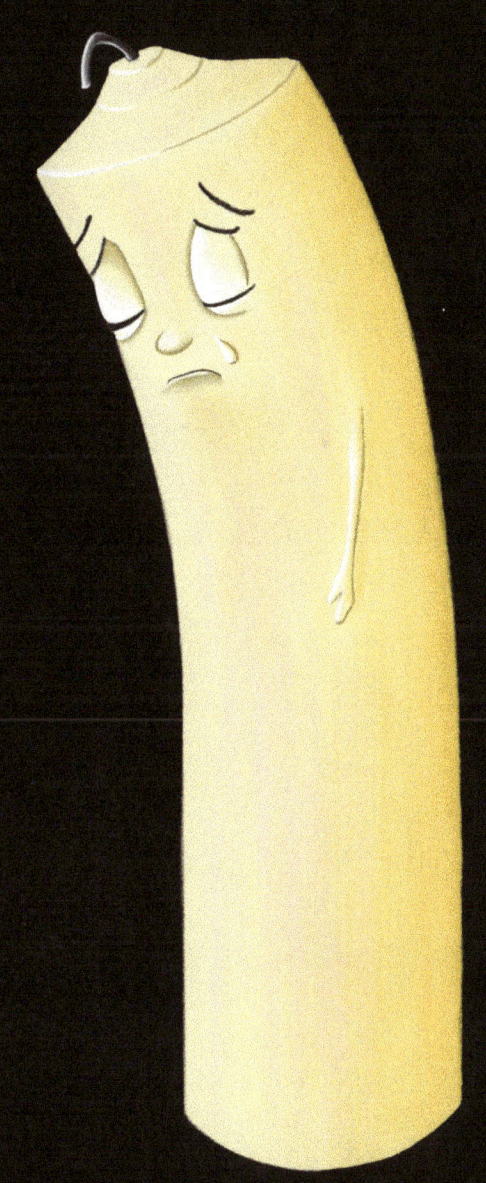

"Well, we can't leave you, can we?" the priest said.

"51."

While the candles bumped around in the box, they imagined their new home. "We shall light dinners!" some said. "No, we shall light a royal wedding!" said others.

The priest placed the box in a closet. When he shut the door, darkness covered them all.

"What are we to do here?" the candles wailed. "This is worse than before! We shall always remain here. Always dark. Always forgotten."

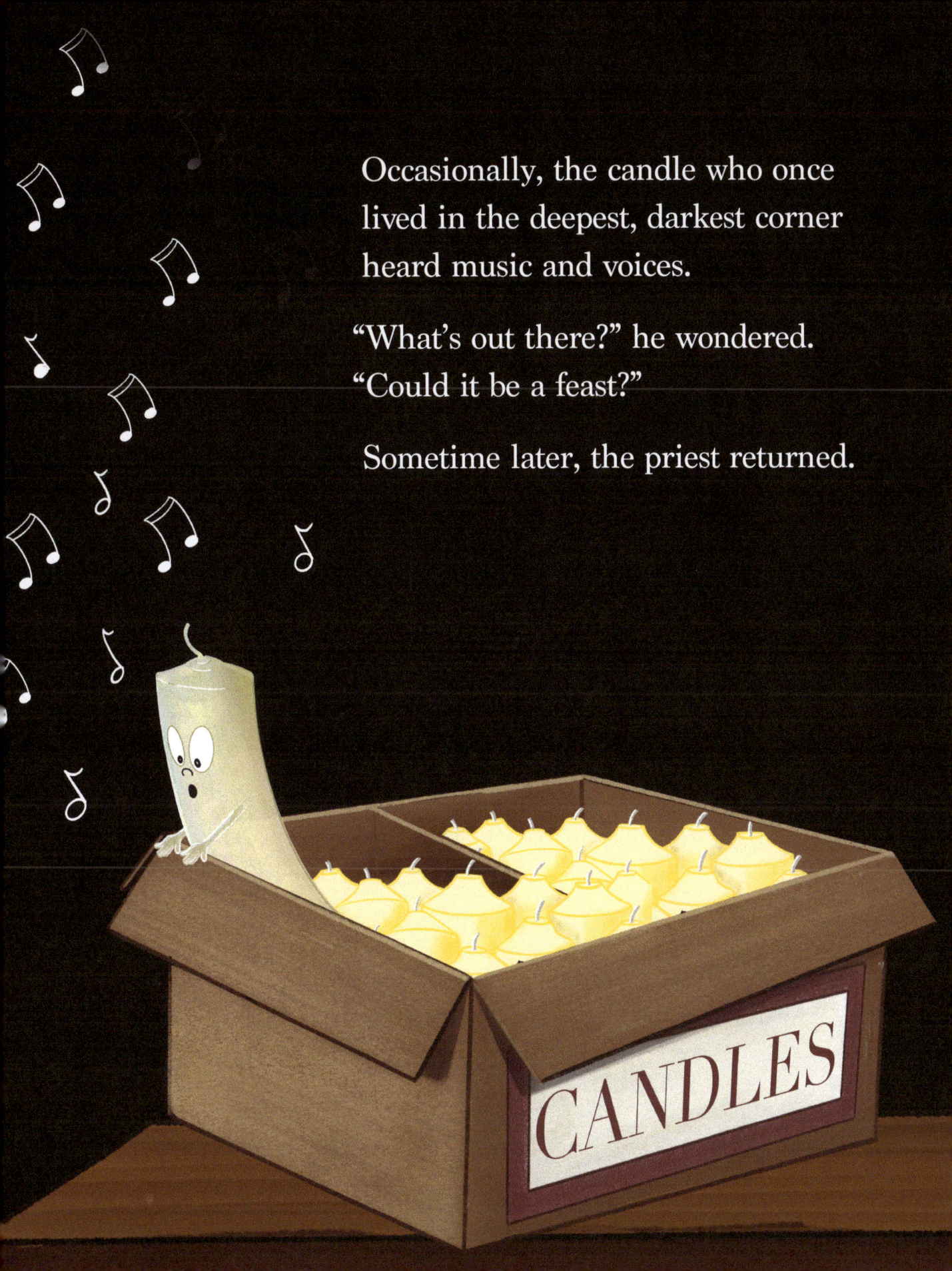

Occasionally, the candle who once lived in the deepest, darkest corner heard music and voices.

"What's out there?" he wondered. "Could it be a feast?"

Sometime later, the priest returned.

He brought four candles, including the candle who once lived in the deepest, darkest corner, to a beautiful table. He lit their wicks.

The candles beamed as flames swayed on their heads for the first time.

The people in the room soon began to sing.

"It's a celebration!" the candle said.

His flame danced with the music.

Then the priest told a story about a man named Jesus who washed the feet of his disciples.

"Jesus," the candle wondered. "Who is he? A king? Why would a king wash someone's feet? Is he a servant?"

The priest taught the people that Jesus loved them and desired to be with each of them. He told them to pray so they could know and love Jesus with all their hearts and minds.

"I want to know and love you, Jesus," the candle thought. "But how? All I've ever wanted was to light a feast."

Finally, the priest approached the table. On it were what appeared to be bread and wine in shining, gold vessels.

"Behold the Lamb of God," he said. "Behold him who takes away the sins of the world. Blessed are those called to the supper of the Lamb."

"A supper!" the candle exclaimed. "So this is a feast!"

The priest gave each person a piece, saying,

"The Body of Christ."

"This is Jesus?" the candle wondered. "Does this Jesus love these people so much that he nourishes them with his body? This isn't just a feast. It's the greatest of feasts!"

For weeks the candle who once lived in the deepest, darkest corner lit the feast. Each day Jesus brought life to all who came.

Every time the candle was lit, he shrunk. Little by little, he melted away. Before his last flame disappeared, he thought of the other candles in the dark closet.

"Be patient and don't despair. You too will light the greatest of feasts. It is a feast celebrating our Lord Jesus, a feast for kings, queens, and servants alike. All are invited, and the music and singing will never end."

Kristina Lahr is a writer and editor in Fargo, North Dakota. She's passionate about fun, wholesome books for all ages. *Candle's Great Feast* is her first book. Visit her online at kristinalahr.com.

Virginia de la Lastra is a physician, illustrator, and apologist. She leads the Chilean Chesterton Society and illustrates for *An Unexpected Journal* and for her medical students, nieces, nephews, and neighbors.

CPSIA information can be obtained
at www.ICGtesting.com
Printed in the USA
BVHW020908250221
601046BV00006B/4